D0817776

Summerland

A Story About Death and Hope

Summerland
A Story About Death and Hope

Eyvind Skeie

Illustrated by Anders Faerevåg
Translated by Hedwig T. Durnbaugh

Brethren Press
Elgin, Illinois

Summerland:
A Story About Death and Hope

Copyright © 1989 by Eyvind Skeie

BRETHREN PRESS, 1451 Dundee Avenue, Elgin, Illinois 60120

Cover design by Jeane Healy
Illustrated by Anders Faerevåg
Translated by Hedwig T. Durnbaugh

Originally published under the title: *Sommerlandet. En fortelling om håp.* Oslo, Norway: Nye Luther Forlag, 1987

Library of Congress Cataloging-in-Publication Data

Skeie, Eyvind, 1947-
    [Sommerlandet. English]
    Summerland: a story about death and hope / Eyvind Skeie; illustrations by Anders Faerevåg; translation by Hedwig T. Durnbaugh.
        p.   cm.
    Translation of: Sommerlandet.
    Summary: A child travels through the Dark Valley which is death and emerges into the Summer Meadow of the afterlife, where she meets Jesus and experiences his comfort and love.
    ISBN 0-87178-824-1
    1. Jesus Christ—Juvenile literature. [1. Death—Fiction. 2. Heaven—Fiction. 3. Jesus Christ—Fiction. 4. Christian life-Fiction.] I. Faerevåg, Anders, ill. II. Title.
PZ7.S6259Su   1989
[E]—dc19   89-7082
                                                  CIP
Manufactured in the United States of America   AC

It was a cold and snowy evening in January. The telephone rang and I heard Anders's voice.

Several years earlier while we were students we had spent much time together. During the following years we had settled in our respective situations and were no longer in such close contact with each other.

Anders and his family live on the island of Røvaer off Haugesund along the west coast of Norway where he is a teacher and free-lance graphic artist. He and his wife Marit have three children.

I knew at once that something was very wrong. Calmly he told me about it.

It had happened two days ago during the forenoon. Five-year-old Ingvil had been alone out of doors sledding in the snow. Most likely the sled had gained too much speed and was out of control so that she went over a precipice, falling and coming to rest among the rocks along the shore. That is where they had found Ingvil.

The doctor arrived in the ambulance helicopter but it was too late to save her life. Ingvil was dead. Left behind were a grieving family who, together, were facing the most heartbreaking of all tasks: to live with sorrow for a lost child, a life not lived, a daughter and sister who no longer would fill the family's days with her presence.

I thought of my own children and the fear all of us parents surely often face, the fear of losing them, the fear that they might be taken from us.

I recalled some of my experiences as pastor, moments of grief and shock that made the world emptier and poorer.

Anders asked me whether I knew of some poem or story, something to share with their other children and which would help them to express both the grief and the hope that is ours.

I knew deep inside that I would try to write something. There is strength in faith and also in our imagination. I tried to write about an innocent child who was walking through a dark valley.

I wrote late into the night keeping the light burning. I was walking in darkness with my story. Then the thought of The One Who Is Waiting came to me. He is the one who bids welcome when all others must say good-bye. Suddenly there was order and coherence.

The next day I mailed the story to the family on Røvaer. I hoped that this word would be a helpful step on the inevitable road of grieving.

On Easter Sunday the story was read on the radio. Letters and telephone calls poured in. The story was copied and sent to people in grief.

The following spring Anders sat down and made the illustrations for this book. I believe that in this way he worked something through within himself.

This is how the story about Summerland came into being.

I hope that it will be read by those who may need some help on their road through the landscape of grieving.

Eyvind Skeie
Oslo, Norway
January, 1986

INGVIL

22/9-79   17/1-85

I do not quite know how to tell you this story, because it is not a fairytale and yet that is exactly what it is. It never happened, yet it is happening all the time. It is about someone you know and at the same time it is not about someone you know.

It is like this. Right beside you there is a valley which you do not see. You do not see it until you are in it, and as long as you are in it, you are not really aware of ever having been there until you are no longer there.

I am talking about the Dark Valley. Some people call it Death but I have always called it the Dark Valley. I call it *valley* because one must go through it, and when you have gone through it you are no longer the way your mommy and daddy, your brothers and sisters, neighbors or friends remember you. You are changed in the Dark Valley and that is what I would like to tell you about.

The Dark Valley is right beside you all the time, only you do not see it. You do not see the Dark Valley until you enter it, and that is when you die.

It is a little difficult to explain this, but when people die, they take a step outside themselves and then they are all at once in the Dark Valley. They have no choice whether they want to go there or not and no one can bring them back from the Dark Valley. The paths in the Dark Valley lead only in one direction. You cannot turn around and go back once you have entered it.

At first there is only darkness in the Dark Valley. Perhaps those who enter it cry a little because it can be scary to be suddenly outside of oneself and in the shadows of the valley.

I say *shadows* because the valley is not completely dark. If it were pitch dark it would be impossible to find one's way through it, but there is a light in the Dark Valley. I shall tell you about that later.

As I said, those who go there may be crying a little at first. But by and by as they walk through the valley, they stop crying. I think that somehow they forget why they are crying. They forget that they have stepped outside of themselves, they forget the bad things that hurt. They only notice that all of a sudden the footpath goes uphill a little. And then they see more and more of the light.

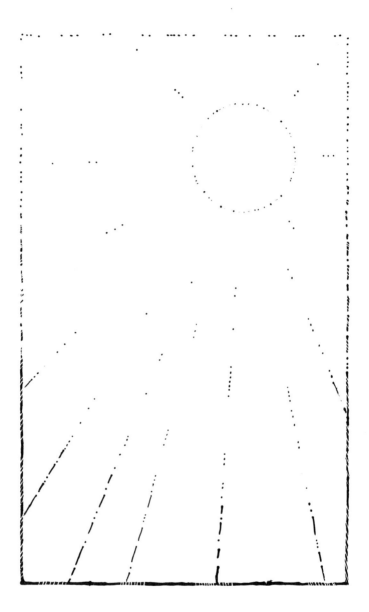

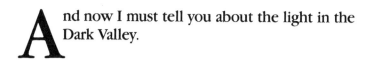

And now I must tell you about the light in the Dark Valley.

But I cannot say anything about the light unless I tell you first about The One Who Is Waiting. That is what I call him, The One Who Is Waiting. I know it is a strange name but I am quite sure that he likes this name better than any other. For that is exactly what he does, he is waiting—always.

At the end of the Dark Valley there is a wide, open meadow. I call this meadow the Summer Meadow, because it is always summer there.

I am sure that to some people it must sound boring that there is always summertime in the Summer Meadow. There are, after all, people who like spring or winter or autumn better than summer.

But in the land that lies beyond the Dark Valley many things are different from the way they are here with us. The seasons of the year do not follow each other in the way you and I are used to. No, in that land the seasons of the year lie side by side. On the one side of the Summer Meadow is the Spring Garden, on the other, a large park called Autumn Orchard, and beyond that you can walk directly into the Winter Forest.

Now in that land you are free to choose the season of the year in which you best like to live. You can walk directly from the Summer Meadow into the Winter Forest or the Spring Garden. And if you are hungry you can take a little walk into the Autumn Orchard and pick a delicious pear or orange. You can do all those things in one single day. And, by the way, in that land there is no night! It is always day.

As I was saying, the Dark Valley opens into the Summer Meadow. I think that is because it is so good to come out into the warm summerland after walking through the shady valley. Right away it makes you feel warm all over.

You can imagine that there are many who feel like lying down and sleeping a while the moment they step into the Summer Meadow. They just lie down in the grass and even if they fall asleep in the brightest sun, their skin does not get sunburned, they just feel very deliciously warm and are dreaming lovely dreams.

But I must not forget to tell you more about The One Who Is Waiting. Because he is the most important part of the story.

He always stands at the far end of the Dark Valley. His eyes are always searching along the shadows because he is waiting for all those who come walking through the valley.

At his side are three angels. These angels are there to help him and they are ready to carry out his wishes.

The first angel is called the Angel with the Light.

Do you know what a lighthouse is, out in the ocean? It is a tower with a light at the top that guides the ships and boats safely into the harbor. Now the Angel with the Light is just like such a lighthouse.

"Come, I hear someone," says The One Who Is Waiting to the Angel with the Light. And then the Angel with the Light walks over to the end of the Dark Valley and shines his light into the darkness.

Those who walk through the valley see the light and know where to go.

"Hush," says The One Who Is Waiting, "I hear the footsteps of a little child. Angel with the Light, send more light! Shine more brightly, show the child the way!"

And every time a little child comes through, the Angel with the Light steps all the way into the Dark Valley. The light is so strong that the shadows disappear and the Dark Valley becomes almost as light as day.

The little child sees the light and hurries towards it.

And then The One Who Is Waiting smiles.

He stretches out his arms towards the child, but the child cannot see it because the light is so bright and the child is still a long way off in the Dark Valley.

Now The One Who Is Waiting calls the second angel. It is the Angel of Hope. Perhaps you do not know what hope is, and so I shall tell you about it. Hope is that which makes you happy and which makes you want to keep going through the Dark Valley.

The One Who Is Waiting knows that the little child may be tired from having walked so far. And so he bids the Angel of Hope come and play his flute.

You see, the Angel of Hope has a flute and when the angel plays music on it, it is as if all the songbirds of the earth were inside that flute. And as the angel plays they come out and fly away carrying his beautiful song with them.

They fly all the way to the child who is walking through the Dark Valley and now the child begins to remember. It remembers the summer and the birds, it remembers that it used to play and jump around in the grass and be happy.

A little while ago I said that when you are in the Dark Valley you cannot turn around and go back. You cannot go back and, therefore, you cannot remember back either.

I know that sounds very strange, but when you cannot remember back you must remember forward and that is exactly what the child does. When it hears the music from the flute and sees the light it remembers forward and then thinks: "I must hurry up and go to where this music is coming from because that is a place where I can be happy, where there is summer and joy."

And now the child begins to run and its feet that had been so tired seem to have been given new strength.

B ut if the child is very small it may not be able to run very far. So, even though the Angel with the Light shines his light as brightly as possible and the Angel of Hope plays his flute as loud and beautifully as possible, the little child may still be too tired to run any more.

Perhaps it sits down to rest and perhaps it even falls asleep.

Do you know what happens then? Let me tell you. The One Who Is Waiting goes into the Dark Valley himself. He is the only one who can go in the opposite direction to meet those who are coming. You see, sometimes even very small children die who have not yet learned to walk. Then The One Who Is Waiting must hurry all the way through the valley to meet them so that he can carry them safely through the Dark Valley and lay them gently down into the grass in the Summer Meadow.

And what do you think he does as he walks through the Dark Valley? He sings! If the child is asleep, he sings lullabies and if it is awake, he sings happy songs about all the things in the Summer Meadow, the Spring Garden, the Winter Forest, and the Autumn Orchard.

T he child can see him come from the same place where the light is. And the child is not a bit afraid nor does it cry because it knows that the one who is coming from the light comes with something good.

And just as The One Who Is Waiting bends down to lift the child up, the child smiles at him. I am almost sure that the child recognizes him even though it has never seen him before. It is as if the child deep inside remembers that someone had lifted it up before, had held it close, that someone far away had loved it and that it had once been in a place where it could sing and play and fall asleep without fear when it was tired.

I think you know where that place is! It is the child's home where it lived until it stepped outside of itself and entered the Dark Valley. Back at the child's home everyone is very sad. They are weeping and mourning. And that is the reason why I must tell you about The One Who Is Waiting.

As I said, he is the one who lifts the child up and carries it in his arms. And I am sure that the child falls sound asleep when that happens. It sleeps and dreams about being carried into the light and laid down in the Summer Meadow. And when it awakes everything will be true because that is exactly what has happened.

The One Who Is Waiting is sitting beside the child. You might also call him The One Who Never Sleeps because he never does, he is always awake. That is because he is waiting for all those who come. That is why he stands where the Dark Valley ends and the Summer Meadow begins. But whenever a little child sleeps in the grass of the Summer Meadow for the first time he sits right beside the child and watches over it even though there is nothing in the meadow that would do the child any harm.

When the child awakes he looks at it and smiles. He strokes its cheeks with his hand that is warm and as light as the wing of a butterfly.

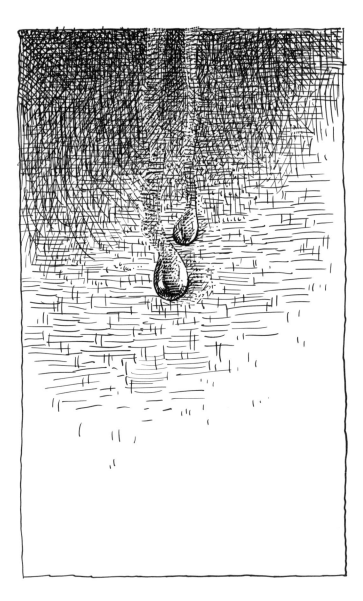

And then the child sees that The One Who Is Waiting weeps. Big tears run down his cheeks. The child can no longer remember what tears are because there is no one in the Summer Meadow who weeps. There is only play and song and joy but, still, the child weeps with The One Who Is Waiting. It weeps although it does not know why.

You and I, we know why the child weeps. It weeps because it no longer is where it used to be—at home with mommy and daddy. But then, of course, the child does not remember that any longer either. It is only we who weep when people we love step outside of themselves and die. Those who have walked through the Dark Valley have somehow left all tears and shadows behind them.

But The One Who Is Waiting remembers how things used to be. He knows about us who live on the other side of the Dark Valley and that is why he weeps with us while he dries the child's tears and makes it smile again.

This is the moment when the third angel comes. The One Who Is Waiting never calls for this angel. It is not necessary because this angel comes every time The One Who Is Waiting weeps. When that happens the angel comes and stands beside The One Who Is Waiting, so close that his tears fall down on the angel. So close that the angel must surely hear the heartbeat of The One Who Is Waiting.

This angel is called the Angel Who Comforts.

The One Who Is Waiting never talks with the Angel Who Comforts. But as soon as the Angel Who Comforts can feel the tears and hear the heartbeat of The One Who Is Waiting, he slowly moves away. The angel moves quietly, ever so quietly that you can barely hear him but when the angel is by your side you may be able to stop weeping after a while. And perhaps one day you will hear the Angel of Hope play music for you, and one night you will perhaps see the Angel with the Light shine even in your dark valley.

After the Angel Who Comforts has left—and I am sure you know where he went—The One Who Is Waiting sits down for a long while beside the child.

I imagine the child climbs up into his lap and perhaps goes back to sleep dreaming for a little while longer before it is finally quite awake.

The One Who Is Waiting looks at the child.

"You are Ingvil," he says, if that is the child's name.

At that moment the child remembers her name. She sits up and smiles and takes the hands of The One Who Is Waiting.

"And you are Jesus," Ingvil says aloud and then lets go of his hands and runs barefoot out into the Summer Meadow.